Islam

&

Christianity

Inter-faith Harmony

Lt Col (r) Parmenas B. Mall

This book is dedicated

To

The Pakistan Army

Contents

About the Author

Lt Col (r) Parmenas B. Mall was born on 30th January 1962 in Sialkot. He got his early education from C.T.I. High school established by United Presbyterian Church and was declared student of the year. After Graduation (B.Sc) from Murray College got commission in the Pakistan Army. Served as a Chief Instructor and Commandant in the Division Battle School. Commanded 60th Battalion (Al-Shuja) and 18th Battalion (The Desert Hawks) the Punjab Regiment (infantry). The author has got Advanced Christian Leadership Training from Haggai Institute Hawaii USA. Retired from the Army in July 2013 and served in Islam Medical and Dental College as an administrator. Married to Prof. Amber Mall presently serving at Forman Christian College Lahore as a Director Admission. Blessed with a daughter and son.

The author is presently living in NJ USA.

Series introduction

Suppose a person is living in an isolated island and he has tasted only bananas in his whole life. Although he has heard about other fruits like mangoes, apples and grapes, he has never tasted them. If he claims that banana is the best fruit on this planet, his claim is not based on any logic or rational because he has never tasted other fruits in this world.

Similarly, people follow the religion of their parents, and they consider that their religion is right and superior, and all other religions are wrong and inferior, without having any knowledge about them. The purpose of this book is to create a positive attitude about other religions and their followers.

The verses from the Holy Quran and the Holy Bible are put together in a logical sequence so that readers can understand both the religions and also pursue righteousness to achieve the ultimate goal of Eternal life. Most people are wasting their precious time in unproductive and worthless issues. We should concentrate in improving our own spiritual life and try to fulfill various obligations and responsibilities which our own religion demands. Some scholars talk less in the favour of their own religion but talk more against other religions. No person has any right to criticize others' faith. Our words and actions should strengthen love not hatred in the society. If a person is hurting others by his words, then he should understand that his words are not from the Almighty God. May God give us wisdom and power to shed away all types of evil and wickedness in our lives and enable us to pursue holiness, goodness and purity which God demands from every human being.

God

In the Holy Quran and in the Holy Bible the concept of one God is very simple and clear. When words like only, alone, and no other God is used, then we should not have any doubt about the oneness of God. In Ex 3:14 God replied to Moses, I am the one who always is; just tell the Israelites, I am has sent me to you. Here we can see words "I am" is used not "we are". However, from the last so many centuries, so called Christian scholars and theologians ignored the Biblical Christianity and formulated own concept about God based on their imaginations and self-created philosophy. And unfortunately various denominations kept on following the same. Verses from the Holy Quran and the Holy Bible will help us to understand the nature of God. Now it is the responsibility of every intellectual, irrespective of his religious background, to find out what is wrong and what is right. I leave it to the reader to ponder and decide. In this era, every person believes what he would like to believe and one person cannot force his own ideas in the minds of others against their will. Most Christian scholars of this era can not explain what they believe and layman Christian does not have enough time to understand their teaching of myth and mysteries. Generally people would like to give their opinion nearly on every issue without reading the Holy books in depth. Our faith should not be based on man made teachings but should be based on verses of the Holy books. Above all, obedience to Almighty God is more important than spending our precious time in discussing the substance of God.

One

Islam: Your God is one God; there is no God except him, the beneficent, and the merciful.

2:163

So believe in Allah and His Apostles: and do not say: Three (Gods) Forbear from saying so: it is best for you verily Allah is only one God.

4:171

Certainly those are infidels who said: "Allah is the third of the three (Gods)." Whereas there is no God except the one God. And if they do not desist (from the blasphemy), then a painful torment will surely befall those who disbelieve from among them.

5:73

And when Allah will ask: O Jesus, son of Mary! Was it you who said to the people: take me and my mother for two gods beside Allah?" He will submit: "Hallowed be you! How dare I say that to which I had no right. If I have said such a thing, you would indeed have known it."

5:116

Your God is one God.

16:22

Lo! Thy Lord is surely one.

37:4

He is Allah the one, the absolute.

39:4

He is Allah's the one, the Almighty.

40:16

Say: He is Allah, the one!

112:1

Christianity: The Lord our God, the Lord is one.

Dt 6:4

He is one who made heaven and earth, the sea, and every thing in them.

Ps 146:6

Teacher of the law asked Jesus, "Of all the commandments, which is the most important?" the most important one," answered Jesus. Is this: "Hear, O Israel, the Lord our God the Lord is one "Well said, teacher." The man replied." You are right in saying that God is one and there is no other but him

Mk 12: 28, 29, 32

There is only one God.

Ro 3.30

There is no God but one.

1Cor 8:4

Yet for us there is but one God, the Father from whom all things came and for whom we live.

1 Co 8:6

There is one Lord, one faith, one baptism, one God and Father of all, who is over all and through all and in all.

Eph 4:5-6

For, there is one God and one mediator between God and men, the man Christ Jesus.

1Ti 2:5

We give thanks to you, Lord God almighty the one who is and who was.

Rev 11:17

Alone

Islam: You alone we worship, and you alone we ask for help.

1:4

Christianity: You alone are the Lord.

Ne 9:6

Why do you call me good? "Christ answered". No one is good except God alone.

Mk 10:18

Who alone is immortal and who lives in unapproachable light, whom no one has seen or can see. To him be honour and might forever.

1Ti 6:16

Only

Islam: The one and only true God and to Him we all surrender ourselves.

2:133

He is only one God.

6:19

We believe in only one Allah.

40:84

Christianity: God the one and only.

Jn 1:18

How can you believe if you accept praise from one another, yet make no effort to obtain the praise that comes from the only God?

Jn 5:44

There is only one God.

Rom 3:30

God, the blessed and only Ruler.

1Ti 6:15

No other God

Islam: Allah (Himself) is witness that there is no God except Him.

3:18

There is no God Save Him.

28:88

There is no God Save Him.

40:3

Christianity: You shall have no other gods before me.

Ex 20:3

I am the first and I am the last; apart from me there is no God.

Isa 44:6

God is one and there is no other but him.

Mk 12:32

Equal

Islam: Nor is there anyone equal to Him.

112:4

Christianity: Who is equal? Says the Holy one.

Isa 40:25

Rivals

Islam: So do not set up rivals to Allah.

22:22

Christianity: Do not bow down to any idol or worship it, because I am the Lord your God and I tolerate no rivals.

Ex 20:5

Alongside

Islam: And cry not unto any other God along with Allah.

28:88

Christianity: Do not make any gods to be alongside me.

Ex 20:23

Besides

Islam: We cry unto no God beside Him.

18:14

Knowest thou not that it is Allah unto whom belongeth the Sovereignty of the heavens and earth; and ye have not, beside Allah any friend or helper?

2:107

Christianity: Worship no God besides me.

Ex 20:3

There is no God besides me.

Dt 32:39

Compare

Islam: And there is none comparable unto Him.

112:4

Christianity: To whom will you compare me or count me equal?

Isa 46:5

Who can be compared with you in majesty?

Ez 31:2

God of Jesus

Islam: And surely Jesus said: "Allah is my Lord as well as your Lord, so worship Him alone. This is the straight path."

19:36

Christianity: Praise be to the God and father of our Lord Jesus Christ.

1Pe 1:3

Jesus said, "I am returning to my Father and you father, to my God and your God."

Jn 20:17

Supreme

Islam: So the power to command is for Allah, the most High, and the supreme.

40:12

Christianity: God is supreme over Christ.

1Cor 10:3

Creator

Islam: Allah is creator of all things.

39:62

Christianity: God, the creator of all things.

Eph 3:9

Eternal

Islam: Allah! There is no God except Him, the Alive, the Eternal.

3:2

Christianity: The Lord, the Eternal God.

Gen 21:33

Almighty

Islam: He is Allah, the one, the Almighty.

40:16

Christianity: O Lord God Almighty, who is like you? You are mighty, O Lord, and your faithfulness surrounds you.

Ps 89:8

Everlasting

Islam: Allah is of infinite bounty.

3:174

Christianity: Stand up and praise the Lord your God, who is from everlasting to everlasting.

Ne 9:5

Most High

Islam: So the power to command is for Allah, the Most High and the Supreme.

40:12

Christianity: I will be glad and rejoice in you, I will sing praise to your name, O Most High.

Ps 9:2

Mighty

Islam: He is the Mighty, the Wise.

14:4

Christianity: For the Mighty one has done great things for me. Holy is his name.

Lk 1:49

Dominant

Islam: And He is Dominant over all His servants. And He is the All-Wise, the All Knowing.

6:18

Christianity: For, dominion belongs to the Lord and he rules over the nations.

Ps 22:8

Sovereign

Islam: Unto Allah belonged the sovereignty of the heavens and the earth.

3:189

Christianity: The Most High is sovereign.

Da 4:25

Ruler

Islam: His is the command, and unto Him you will be brought back.

28:88

Christianity: God, the blessed and only Ruler, the King of kings and Lord of lords.

1Ti 6:15

Throne

Islam: There is no God except Him. In Him have I put my trust and He is Lord of the Tremendous Throne.

9:129

Christianity: God is seated on his holy throne.

Ps 47:8

Your throne, O God, will last for ever.

Ps 45:6

Partners

Islam: Set not up with Allah any other God (O man) lest thou sit down reproved forsaken.

17:22

And serve Allah. Ascribe nothing as partner unto Him.

4:36

Make none sharer of the worship due unto his Lord.

18:110

Christianity: Do not make any gods to be alongside me.

Ex 20:23

You shall have no other gods before me.

Ex 20:3

Comparison

Islam: And there is none comparable unto Him.

112:4

Christianity: To whom, then, will you compare God?

Isa 40:18

All things

Islam: Lo! You are able to do all things.

66:8

Christianity: I know that you can do all things.

Job 42:2

All-knowing

Islam: And He is Dominant over all His servants. And He is the All-wise, the All-knowing.

6:18

Christianity: Do not keep talking so proudly or let your mouth speak such arrogance, for the Lord is a God who knows and by him deeds are weighed.

1Sam 2:3

Belongs to the Lord

Islam: Unto him belong whatsoever is in the heavens and whatsoever is in the earth.

2:255

Christianity: Everything under heaven belongs to me.

Job 41:11

The whole earth is mine.

Ex 19:5

Wise

Islam: There is no God save Him, the Almighty, the wise.

3:18

Christianity: To God, who alone is wise, be the glory for ever.

Ro 16:27

Friend

Islam: God is your protecting friend. A Blessed patron and a Blessed Helper.

22:78

Christianity: Friendship with the Lord is reserved for those who fear him.

Ps 25:14

Protector

Islam: But Allah is your protector and He is the Best of helpers.

3:150

Christianity: For the Lord loves the just and will not forsake his faithful ones. They will be protected forever, but offspring of the wicked will be cut off.

Ps 37:28

Helper

Islam: If Allah is your helper none can overcome you, and if He withdraws his help from you, who is there who can help you.

3:160

Christianity: Lord is my helper, I will not be afraid. What can man do to me?

Heb 13:6

Merciful

Islam: Your God is one God; there is no God except him, the Beneficent, the Merciful.

2:163

Christianity: Yet he was merciful; he forgave their iniquities and did not destroy them. Time after time he restrained his anger and did not stir up his full wrath.

Ps 78:38

Kind

Islam: Allah is a Lord of kindness to (His) creatures.

2: 251

Christianity: Do you show contempt for the riches of his kindness, tolerance and patience, not realizing that God's kindness leads you towards repentance?

Ro 2:4

Mary

Islam: And when the angels said: O Mary! Lo! Allah has chosen you and made you pure and has preferred you above (all) the women of creation.

3:42

Christianity: The angel went to Mary and said "Greetings, you who are highly favoured! The Lord is with you." From now on all generation will call me blessed.

Lk 1:28,48

Distinguished birth (Christ)

Islam: She (Mary) said: My Lord! How can I have a child when no mortal has touched me? He said: so (it will be). Allah createth what He will. If He decreeth a thing, He saith unto it only: Be! And it is.

3:47

Christianity: "How will this be," Mary asked the angel, "since I am a virgin?" The angel answered, "The Holy Spirit will come upon you, and the power of the Most High will overshadow you. So, the holy one to be born will be called the Son of God.

Lk 1:34,35

Faultless

Islam: Mary said Lo! I seek refuge in the Beneficent One from thee, if thou art God fearing. He (Angel) said: I am only a messenger of thy Lord that I may bestow on thee a faultless son (Jesus).

19:18, 19

Christianity: Christ committed no sin and no deceit was found in his mouth.

1Pe 2:22

Blessed

Islam: He (Jesus) spoke: Lo! I am the slave of Allah. He hath given me the scripture and hath appointed me a prophet. And hath made me blessed.

19:30:31

Christianity: Elizabeth was filled with the Holy Spirit. In a loud voice she exclaimed: Blessed are you among women, and blessed is the child you will bear.

Lk 1:41-42

Childhood

Islam: (And it was said unto his son): O John! Hold fast the scripture. And we gave Him (Jesus) wisdom when a child.

19:12

Christianity: Christ (at the age of twelve) was in the Temple, sitting among the religious teachers, discussing deep questions with them. And all who heard him were amazed at his understanding and his answers.

Lk 2:46-47

Obedient

Islam: And he (Jesus) was dutiful to his parents, and was not insolent, disobedient.

19:14

Christianity: Then Jesus went down to Nazareth with them (parents) and was obedient to them.

Lk 2:51

Wisdom

Islam: And He (God) will teach him (Christ) the scripture and wisdom and the Torah and the Gospel.

3:48.

Christianity: And Jesus grew in wisdom and stature and in favour with God and men.

Lk 2:52

Holy Spirit

Islam: When Allah Saith: O Jesus, son of Mary! Remember My favour onto you and unto your mother, how I strengthened you with the holy spirit.

5:110

Christianity: God anointed Jesus Christ with the Holy Spirit and power, and how he went around doing good and healing all who were under the power of the devil, because God was with him.

Ac 10:38

Pure

Islam: And (we) granted him (Jesus) tenderness of heart from our presence and purity of self. And he was most God fearing.

19:13 23

Christianity: Christ is pure.

1Jn 3:3

Righteous

Islam: He (Jesus) is of the righteous.

3:46

A prophet (Jesus), of the righteous.

3:39

Christianity: Christ is righteous.

1Jn 3:7

Can any of you prove me guilty of sin?

Jn 8:46

Light

Islam: And we gave to him (Jesus) the Gospel in which there was guidance and Light.

5:46

Christianity: You have the words of eternal Life.

Jn 6:68

The unfolding of your words gives Light.

Ps 119:130

Miracles

Islam: And you (Jesus) did heal him who was born blind and the leper by my permission and how you did raise the dead by my permission.

5:110

Christianity: Lazarus was raised from the dead.

Jn 11:1-45

Jesus healed a man born blind.

Jn 9:1-7

Ten lepers were healed.

Lk17:11-19

Signs

Islam: We gave Jesus, Son of Mary, clear signs and we strengthened him with the Holy Spirit.

2 : 87

And, when Jesus came, with clear signs.

43 : 63

Christianity: A great crowd of people followed him because they saw the miraculous signs he had performed on the sick.

Jn 6:2

Jesus disciples saw Christ do many other miraculous signs besides the ones recorded in this book.

Jn 20:30

People of Israel, God publicly endorsed Jesus of Nazareth by doing wonderful miracles, wonders and signs through him as you well know.

Ac 2:22

Exalted

Islam: Of those messengers, some of whom We have caused to excel others, and of whom there are some unto whom Allah spake, while some of them He exalted (above others) in degree; and we gave Jesus son of Mary, clear proofs (of Allah's sovereignty) and we supported him with the Holy Spirit.

2:253

Christianity: Therefore, God exalted Christ to the highest place and gave him the name that is above every name.

Php 2:9

The Spirit of the Lord is on me (Christ) because he has anointed me to preach good news to the poor.

Lk 4:18

Ascended

Islam: But Allah took him (Jesus) up unto himself.

4:158

Christianity: When Christ was blessing them, he left them and was taken up to heaven.

Lk 24:51

With the Lord

Islam: Recall, when the angels said: 'O Mary! Allah gives you the glad tidings of a command from Him. His name shall be messiah Jesus son of Mary, illustrious in the world and the Hereafter and shall be of those brought near to Allah.

3:45

Recall, when Allah said," O Jesus! I shall cause you to attain your full term of life, and I am about to raise you towards myself.

3:55

Christianity: Stephen, filled with the Holy Spirit, looked up to heaven and saw the glory of God with Jesus standing at God's right hand.

Ac 7:56

Our high priest (Christ) sat down in the place, of highest honour in heaven, at God's right hand.

Heb 8:1

Repentance

Islam: The repentance, acceptance of which Allah has undertaken is of those who commit a sin in foolishness and thereafter repent forthwith. So these are the people to whom Allah turns (in mercy), and verily Allah is the All knowing, the All wise.

4:17

Christianity: God had granted even the gentiles repentance into life.

Ac 11:18

Each of you must turn from wicked ways and reform your actions.

Jer 35:15

Turn to God

Islam: Truly Allah loves those who turn unto Him.

2:222

Christianity: Repent, then and turn to God, so that your sins may be wiped out, that time of refreshing may come from Lord.

Ac 3:19

Evil

Islam: Gardens of Eden which they enter, underneath which rivers flow, herein they have what they will. Thus Allah repayeth those who ward off (evil).

16:31

Christianity: Avoid every kind of evil.

1Th 5:22

Immorality

Islam: You enjoin (instruct) right conduct and forbid indecency.

3:110

Squander (waste) not (your wealth) in wantonness (immorality)

17:26

Christianity: Make sure that no one is immoral or godless.

Heb 12:16

Do not get drunk on wine, which leads to debauchery (immorality).

Eph 5:18

Adultery

Islam: And do not go near adultery, surely it is a great obscenity. And a most evil path.

17:32

Christianity: Do not commit adultery.

Mk 10:19

Lewdness

Islam: Say; Allah, verily, enjoined (instruct) not lewdness.7:28

The devil promised you destitution and enjoined on you lewdness.

2:268

Christianity: Now your impurity is lewdness.

Ez 24:13

Let there be no sexual immorality, impurity or greed among you. Such sins have no place among God's people.

Eph 5:3

Wine

Islam: That is what Satan wants to sow enmity and hatred among you by means of wine and gambling, and keep you from the remembrance of Allah and from prayer. Are you not then going to desist?

5:91

Christianity: Wine is a mocker and beer a brawler, whoever is led astray by them is not wise.

Pr 20:1

Interest

Islam: O you who believe! Do not devour interest by doubling and redoubling it, and keep fearing Allah that perhaps you may prosper.

3:130

Christianity: He does not lend at usury or take excessive interest. That man is righteous; he will surely live, declares the sovereign Lord.

Ez 18:8,9

Unjust

Islam: And so far those are who are unjust they are firewood for hell.

72:15

Christianity: Woe to him who builds his realm by unjust gain to set his nest on high to escape the clothes of ruin!

Hab 2:9

Scales

Islam: A give full measure when you measure out anything and weigh with even balance. That is the better way and has a good result as well.

17:35

Christianity: The Lord abhors (reject) dishonest scales, but accurate weights are his delight.

Pr 11:1

Speech

Islam: Allah loveth not the utterance of harsh speech.

4:148

Christianity: Get rid of all bitterness, rage, anger, harsh words and slander as well as all types of malicious behavior.

Eph 4:31

Conversation

Islam: Successful indeed are the believers, and who shun vain conversation.

23:1,3

Christianity: A gossip betrays a confidence; so avoid a man who talks too much.

Pr 20:19

Slander

Islam: And if a slander from the devil wound thee, then seek refuge in Allah. Lo! He is Hearer, knower.

7:200

Christianity: Do not go about spreading slander among your people. Do not do anything that endangers your neighbor's life.

Lev 19:16

Mock

Islam: O you who believe! Let not a folk deride (mock) a folk who may be better than they (are) nor women (deride) women who may be better than they are.

49:11

Christianity: If you are wise your wisdom will reward you if you are a mocker you alone will suffer.

Pr 9:12

Fools mock at making amends for sin but goodwill is found among the upright.

Pr 14:9

Lies

Islam: The curse of Allah upon those who lie.

3:61

Christianity: Do not lie to each other.

Col 3:9

Insult

Islam: Neither defames one another, nor insults one another by nicknames. Bad is the name of lewdness after faith.

49:11

Christianity: Do not repay evil with evil or insult with insult, but with blessings, because to this you were called so that you may inherit blessings.

1Pe 3:9

Hypocrisy

Islam: Allah has promised the hypocrites, men and women, and the disbelievers the fire of hell, abiding therein for ever.

9:68

Christianity: Therefore, rid yourselves of all malice (enmity) and all deceit, hypocrisy, envy (jealousy) and slander (backbiting) of every kind.

1Pr 2:1

Thoughts

Islam: O you who believe! If ye keep your duty to Allah, He will give you discrimination (between right and wrong) and will rid you of your evil thoughts and deeds and will forgive you.

8:29

Christianity: O Jerusalem, wash the evil from your heart and be saved. How long will you harbour wicked thoughts?

Jer 4:14

Pride

Islam: Lo! Allah love not such as are proud and boastful.

4:36

Christianity: God opposes the proud but gives grace to the humble.

Ja 4:6

Wicked

Islam: And lo! The wicked verily will be in hell.

82:14

Christianity: I, the Lord will punish the world for its evil and the wicked for their sin.

Isa 13:11

Satan

Islam: O mankind! Eat of what is in the earth lawful and wholesome, and do not follow the footsteps of Satan verily he is to you an open enemy. And he only commands you to commit evil and indecency and to assert falsely about Allah what you know nothing of.

2:168,169

Christianity: Be self-controlled and alert, your enemy, the devil prowls around like a roaring lion looking for someone to devour (swallow). Resist him and be firm in your faith.

1Pet 5:8,9

Stand against the devil schemes.

Eph 6:11

World

Islam: You desire the goods of the world and Allah desires

(for you) the Hereafter.

8:67

O my people! Lo! This life of the world is but a passing comfort, and lo! The Hereafter, that is the enduring home.

40:39

Christianity: Do not love the world or anything in the world. If anyone loves the world, the love of the God is not in him. 1Jn 2:15 Any one who chooses to be a friend of the world becomes an enemy of God.

Jam 4:4

Forgiveness

Islam: Forgiveness is only incumbent on Allah toward those who do evil in ignorance (and) then turn quickly (in repentance) to Allah. These are they toward whom Allah relenteth. Allah is ever knower, wise.

4:17

Christianity: If my people, who are called by my name, will humble themselves and pray and seek my face and turn from their wicked ways, then will I hear from heaven and will forgive their sin.

2Chr 7:14

Forgive others

Islam: And we prescribed for them therein. The life for the life and the eye for the eye and the nose for the nose and the ear for the ear and the tooth for the tooth and for wounds retaliation. But whoso forget it (in the way of charity) it shall be expiation for him.

5:45

Christianity: You have heard that it was said, "Eye for eye, and tooth for tooth". But I tell you, do not resist an evil person. If some one strikes you on the right cheek, turn to him the other also. Mt 5:38, 39

Forgive and you will be forgiven.

Lk 6:37

Path

Islam: Show us the straight path.

1:5

Christianity: Lead me in a straight path.

Ps 27:11

Light

Islam: Lo! We did reveal the Torah wherein is guidance and a light.

5:44

Christianity: The unfolding of your words gives light it gives understanding to the simple.

Ps 119:130

Purify

Islam: Therein are men who like to remain purified and clean. And Allah loves those who are clean and pure.

9:108

Christianity: Dear friends, let us purify ourselves from every thing that contaminates body and spirit, perfecting holiness out of reverence for God.

2Co 7:1

Darkness to light

Islam: He may bring forth those who believe and do good works from darkness unto light.

65:11

Christianity: For, you were once darkness, but now you are light in the Lord. Live as children of light.

Eph 5:8

Righteous

Islam: The righteous man is he who ward off (evil).

2:189

Christianity: He who does what is right is righteous, just as he (God) is righteous.

1Jn 3:7

Fear of the Lord

Islam: O people! Fear your Lord; verily the tremor of the Hour (of Resurrection) is a thing most severe.

22:1

Christianity: He who fears the Lord is a fountain of life turning a man from the snares of death.

Pr 14:27

Obedience

Islam: Keep your duty to Allah and obey me.

3:50

Christianity: We must obey God.

Ac 5:29

Conduct

Islam: Lo! The noblest of you, in the sight of Allah is the best in conduct.

49:13

Christianity: And we are instructed to turn from godless and sinful pleasures. We should live in this evil world with self- control and devotion to God.

Tit 2:12

Doing right

Islam: For such of them as do right and ward off (evil), there is great reward.

3:172

Christianity: Stop doing wrong, learn to do right.

Is 1:16,17

Good works

Islam: So vie (compete) with one another in good works.

2:148

Christianity: All scripture is God breathed and is useful for teaching, rebuking, correcting and training in righteousness, so that man of God may be thoroughly equipped for every good work.

2Tim 3:16,17

Goodness

Islam: Those who followed them in goodness - Allah is well pleased with them and they are well pleased with Him.

9:100

Christianity: Hate what is evil, cling to what is good.

Ro 12:9

Wisdom

Islam: He bestows wisdom upon whom He will, and whoso-ever is granted wisdom he is indeed granted abundant good, and none accepts admonition except of understanding.

2:269

Christianity: For the Lord gives wisdom and from his mouth come knowledge and understanding.

Pr 2:6

Blessed is the man who finds wisdom.

Pr 3:13

Peace

Islam: Lo! He (Allah) loves not the aggressors.

7:55

Christianity: When you march up to attack a city, make its people an offer of peace.

Dt 20:10

Neighbour

Islam: (Show) kindness onto the neighbour who is of kin (unto you) and the neighbour who is not of kin.

4:36

Christianity: Love your neighbour as yourself.

Lk 10:27

Kindness

Islam: And Forget not kindness among yourselves.

2:237

Christianity: Always try to be kind to each other, and to every one else.

1Th 5:15

Generosity

Islam: The alms (charitable donation) are only for the poor and the needy.

9:60

Christianity: Give generously to others in need.

Eph 4:28

Justice

Islam: My Lord enjoins (command) justice.

7:29

Christianity: Learn to do right! Seek justice encourage the oppressed.

Isa 1:17

Doing Good

Islam: Spend your wealth for the cause of Allah, and be not cast by your own hands to ruin and do good. Lo! Allah love the beneficent.

2:195

Christianity: Therefore, as we have opportunity, let us do good to all people.

Gal 6:10

Parents

Islam: We have enjoined on man kindness to parents.

29:8

Christianity: Children, obey your parents in every thing, for this pleases the Lord.

Col 3:20

Children

Islam: (Show) Kindness unto near kindred.

4:36

Christianity: Fathers, do not embitter your children, or they will become discouraged.

Col 3:21

Modesty

Islam: And tell the believing women to lower their gaze and be modest.

24:31

Christianity: I also want women to dress modesty, with decency and propriety, not with braided hair or gold or pearls or expensive clothes but with good deeds.

1Ti 2:9, 10

Humble

Islam: And seek help through patience and prayer, and without doubt prayer is an exacting discipline but not (hard) to those who are humble and God fearing.

2:45

Christianity: God opposes the proud but gives grace to the humble.

1Pe 5:5

For whoever exalts himself will be humbled and whoever humbles himself will be exalted.

Mt 23:12

Cleanness

Islam: Truly Allah loves those who have a care for cleanness.

2:222

Christianity: The Lord has dealt with me according to my righteousness; according to the cleanness of my hand he has rewarded me.

Ps 18:20

Eating

Islam: Eat of that which Allah hath bestowed on you as food lawful and good.

5:88

Christianity: Eat what is good, and your soul will delight in the richest of fare.

Isa 55:2

Prayers

Islam: Be guardians of your prayers and of the midmost prayer and stand up with devotion to Allah.

2:238

Christianity: Devote yourselves to prayer, being watchful and thankful.

Col. 4:2

Worship

Islam: And your Lord has commanded that you should worship none but Him alone.

17:23

You alone we worship and you alone we ask for help.

1:4

Christianity: Worship the Lord your God.

Lk 4:8

Thankful

Islam: Allah will reward the thankful.

3:144

Christianity: Give thanks in all circumstances.

1Th 5:18

Serve the Lord

Islam: O my people! Serve Allah, ye have no other God save Him.

11:84

Christianity: Worship the Lord your God, and serve him only.

Mt 4:10

Steadfast

Islam: Allah is with the steadfast.

8:66

Christianity: You will keep in perfect peace him whose mind is steadfast.

Is 26:3

Guardian

Islam: He is guardian over all things.

39:62

Christianity: For, he will command his angels concerning you to guard you in all your ways.

Ps 91:11

Watch

Islam: There are degrees (of grace and reprobation) with Allah, and Allah is seer of what you do.

3:163

Christianity: For the Lord watches over the way of the righteous, but the way of the wicked will perish.

Ps 1:6

Success

Islam: These depend on guidance from their Lord. These are the successful.

2:5

Christianity: Be strong and very courageous. Be careful to obey all the law my servant Moses gave you, do not turn from it to the right or to the left, that you may be successful wherever you go.

Jos 1:7

Humbles and Exalts

Islam: You exalt whom you will, and you abase whom you will.

3:26

Christianity: The Lord sends poverty and wealth, he humbles and he exalts.

1Sa 2:7

Return

Islam: Then unto your Lord is your return.

6:165

Christianity: The dust returns to the ground it came from and the spirit returns to God who gave it.

Ecc 12:7

Gathered

Islam: He (God) it is unto whom ye will be gathered.

6:72

Christianity: Therefore wait for me; declares the Lord, for the day I will stand up to testify. I have decided to assemble the nations, to gather the Kingdoms.

Zep 3:8

Judgment

Islam: The day, when we gather the righteous to the presence of the Lord Most- kind as honoured guests - And (on that day) drive the guilty to hell like thirsty beasts.

19:85, 86

Christianity: Angels will weed out of his kingdom everything that causes sin and all who do evil. They will throw them in to the fiery furnace where there will be weeping and gnashing of teeth. Then the righteous will shine like the sun in the kingdom of their father.

Mt 13:41-43

Escape

Islam: You cannot escape (from Him) in the earth or in the sky.

29:22

Christianity: Do you think you will escape God's judgment?

Ro 2:3

Hell

Islam: Lo! the guilty are immortal in hells torment.

43:74

Christianity: But the cowardly, the unbelieving, the vile, the murderers, the sexually immoral, those who practice magic arts, the idolaters and all liars - their place will be in the fiery lake of burning sulfur. This is second death.

Rev 21:8

Sharing

Islam: Whosoever goeth right it is only for (the good of) his own soul that goeth right and whosoever erreth, erreth only to its hurt . No laden soul can bear another's load.

17:15

Christianity: The soul who sins is the one who will die. The son will not share the guilt of the father, nor will the father share the guilt of the son. The righteousness of righteous man will be credited to him and the wickedness of the wicked will be charged against him.

Ez 18:20

Impartial

Islam: Take it for granted, that whether it be the followers of Islam or the Jews or the Christians or the Sabians-whosoever believe in Allah and the Last day and work righteous deeds - surely their reward is with their Lord; they shall have nothing to fear, nor shall they grieve.

2:62

Christianity: Many, I (Jesus) tell you, will come from east and west to sit down with Abraham, Isaac, and Jacob at the feast in the kingdom of heaven. But those who were born to the kingdom will be thrown out in to the dark, where there will be weeping and grinding of teeth.

Mt 8:11-12

Favouritism

Islam: Lo! Those who believe, and those who are Jews and Sabaeans, and Christians - whosoever believeth in Allah and the Last Day and doth right, there shall no fear come upon them neither shall they grieve.

5:69

And whatever good they (people of scripture) do, they will not be denied the meed (reward) thereof.

3:115

Christianity: Then Peter began to speak, I now realize how true it is that God does not show favouritism, but accepts men from every nation who fear him and do what is right.

Ac 10:34,35

For God does not show favouritism.

Ro 2:11

Good

Islam: Lo! The mercy of Allah is nigh unto the good.

7:56

Christianity: The Lord approves of those who are good, but he condemns those who plan wickedness.

Pr 12:2

Reward

Islam: So Today no soul will be wronged in the least, nor will be rewarded but for what you used to do.

36:54

Christianity: He will judge or reward you according to what you do.

1Pe 1:17

Irrespective of our religious background, we should try to act upon these verses to improve our conduct, rather than wasting time in finding faults and errors in other religions. We can learn valuable and important lessons from every religion of this world. Let us pray to God that he may forgive our sins and give us wisdom and power to live according to his will. May God bless all of us.

Author's email:mall_62@hotmail.com